# Groovy Girls™
## Sleep Over Club

# Choose or Lose
## How to Pick a Winner

Vote for Reese!

Vote for Oki!

### Robin Epstein

Scholastic Inc.

New York  Toronto  London  Auckland  Sydney
Mexico City  New Delhi  Hong Kong  Buenos Aires

# Read all the books about the Groovy Girls!

To Aunt Ros,
a perfect example of style and grace!

Cover illustration by Taia Morley
Interior illustrations by Bill Alger, Doug Day, Elaine de la Mata,
Yancey Labat, and Kurt Marquart

ISBN 0-439-81435-9

The Groovy Girls™ books are produced under license from Manhattan Group, LLC.
Go to groovygirls.com for more Groovy Girls fun!

12 11 10 9 8 7 6 5 4 3 2 1          5 6 7 8 9 10/0
Printed in the U.S.A.
First Little Apple printing, September 2005

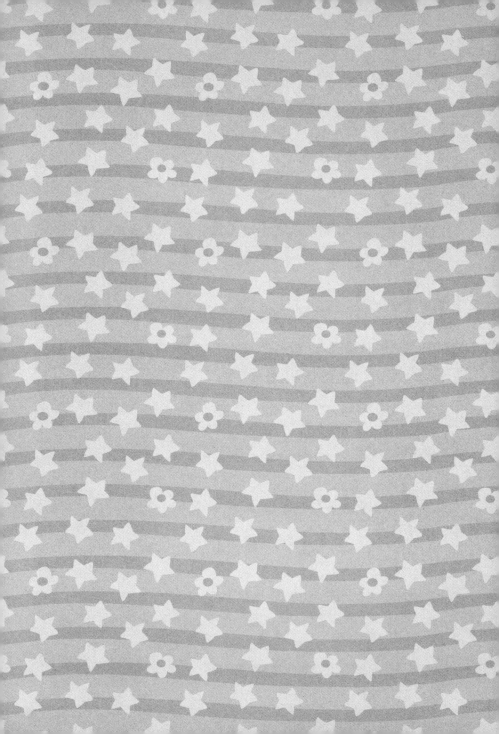

## Chapter 1

# The Big Ta-Da!

"I've made a huge, woolly-mammoth whopper of a decision," Reese McCloud announced to her twin sister, O'Ryan, as the girls walked home from school one afternoon.

"Cool, I have, too!" O'Ryan replied, taking a flying leap over a giant puddle. "I'm gonna start speaking in *Ig-pay Atin-lay* all the *ime-tay*."

"Speaking in Pig Latin? You think *that's* a decision of woolly-mammoth huge-i-tude?" Reese replied, rolling her eyes.

"Es-yay!" O'Ryan nodded, hopping over another puddle.

"Well, I'm gonna run for school treasurer!" Reese said, throwing her arms out to her sides, as if she'd just pulled off a neat magic trick.

Now it was O'Ryan's turn to roll her eyes. "School treasurer?" she said, shaking her head. "*That's* what you call a big decision?"

"Totally!" Reese replied. "Because it is."

"But being a treasurer is boring," O'Ryan said. "I mean, like, you have to do all that math-y junk. Why would you choose to do that on *purpose*?"

"Well, first of all," Reese said, holding up her pointer finger to count out the first reason, "I've always been a whiz with dough."

"You're a baker?"

"I'm saying, I'm good with moolah," Reese explained. "Cool with cash. I mean, don't you remember last summer when I saved up all my allowance and wallpapered the wall behind my bed with all those dollar bills?"

"Sure," O'Ryan nodded, picturing the wall of Washingtons.

"Well?" Reese said, as if her point was obvious.

"Well, *what*?"

"How many people do you know who've done that?"

"How many people would *want* to?" O'Ryan replied, trying hard not to laugh. "I just think it's *razy-cay*!"

"Hang on! I'm not done listing my reasons yet," Reese continued, now holding up her middle finger to join her pointer. "So, second of all, in addition to being good with money, I also have some really great ideas for what to sell in the school store."

"You do?" O'Ryan asked, surprised her sister had gotten this far in her thinking.

"You know how they just sell, like, pens and pencils and school supply stuff now?" Reese said. "Well, I think it would be totally supreme to stock the store with other stuff that kids really want, too."

"Like what?"

"Like cute, scented erasers," Reese replied, unzipping the front pocket of her backpack and pulling out a puppy-shaped eraser that looked a lot like their dog, Sleepless.

O'Ryan took the eraser from Reese and put it right up to her nose. "Mmmm, I *ove-lay* these things!" she said.

"*And* I'd also sell different colors and flavors of lip gloss," Reese said.

"Yeah! I would totally buy them," O'Ryan replied excitedly.

"*Plus*, I'd order gross things that boys like, too!" Reese added. "You know, like little robots and stuff that's made out of mud and sticks and whatever."

"Hmmm," O'Ryan nodded. "That *is* kinda smart."

"And, my third reason for running for treasurer," Reese said, holding up her third finger and making it look like she was doing a Girl Scout pledge, "is that I already know how to do it."

"How's that?"

"Well, we've watched Mom sell stuff at 'Hey Betty' for years and years. I mean, the two of us practically run the store already."

"That's so true!" O'Ryan agreed. "I can't believe it, but I actually think you just managed to change my mind."

Then O'Ryan paused for a moment, realizing her sister hadn't only made her think differently about the treasurer business, but she'd inspired her, too.

"And I just got a majorly brilliant brainstorm!" O'Ryan shouted. "I can be your campaign manager!"

"Uh," Reese replied, not sounding nearly as inspired by this idea as her twin. "I don't know about that."

"What do you mean, you don't know?" O'Ryan asked. "I'd be Captain Campaign-errific."

"Well," Reese said slowly, "I mean, being a campaign manager is a lot of work. You have to keep things running in perfect order. And if your side of our room is any clue, perfect order isn't exactly your strength."

It was true. O'Ryan's side of the girls' shared bedroom looked like a pigsty.

(No, wait…a pig might get upset by a comparison like that! So let's just say O'Ryan's side of the room was so sloppy, sometimes it was hard to find her bed!)

"Hold on!" O'Ryan replied. "I can keep things running smoothly if I really want to."

Reese folded her arms in front of her, not looking convinced. "Really?" she said.

"Totally. Um, okay, like…" O'Ryan started racking her brain for examples. "Oh! Here's one!" she said, sticking up her pointer finger. "When I was in charge of handing out orange slices at soccer practice, that always went really well."

"That's true," Reese nodded.

"Ooh, and here are two more," O'Ryan added, holding up her second and third fingers. "I always water the plants on the front porch before they start to droop. *And,* I change the water in Sleepless's bowl every morning!"

As Reese listened to these examples, she started to change her mind. "Well, if you really think you can put your mind to it," she said.

"Are you kidding? Of *course* I can," O'Ryan replied. "I'll do whatever it takes to make sure you get elected. You're my best sister, after all. And I think you'd make the most super-supreme school treasurer imaginable!"

"Well, okay—if you're sure," Reese replied.

"Of course I'm sure. I'm pledge-of-allegiance sure. I'm pinky-promise sure. I'm 100-percent pure sure!" O'Ryan said, raising both of her arms in the air and wiggling all ten fingers.

"Wow!" Reese replied, starting to warm up to the idea's greatness. "You know, if the two of us put our heads together, we really *could* run the grooviest campaign the school has ever seen."

"That's right! With the McCloud team running together, nothing will stand in our way," O'Ryan assured her.

Reese chuckled.

"What?" O'Ryan asked.

"Know what would have been funny? If you'd decided to run for treasurer, too."

"Yikes!" O'Ryan said with a laugh. "That woulda been *ragic-tay*. I mean, can you imagine if the two of us ran against each other? That would be like asking people to choose between jelly beans and Skittles. Between Kit Kats and 100 Grand bars. Between Starbursts and Blow Pops! How could you even begin to make such a hard choice?"

"Well, thank goodness we'll never ask them to do that!" Reese said, pulling her best sis and fave twin into a huge hug.

"And that's a fact you can take to the piggy *ank-bay*!" O'Ryan replied.

## Chapter 2

# Tied Up in Knots

"Ow, ow, ow, ow," O'Ryan yowled. She was sitting on the floor in Oki's bedroom as Oki sat on the bed behind her, French braiding her hair.

"That didn't hurt!" Oki replied, taking another strand of hair. "Come on. I bet it even felt good."

"Since when does getting hair yanked out of your head feel good?" O'Ryan asked. She tried turning around to see Oki, but as she turned, the braid twisted tighter. "Yow!" she yelped again.

O'Ryan had gone to Oki's house that night so the girls could watch their favorite TV show together, *Fashion 411*.

"Sorry about that," Oki replied, still gripping O'Ryan's braid like a tug-of-war rope, "but sometimes you've got to suffer for beauty!"

"Like that?" O'Ryan said, pointing to the TV where a model was trying to zip herself into a pair of jeans that were clearly two sizes too small.

"Yeah, but when I open my own boutique when I'm older, I won't just sell tight jeans. I plan to stock lots of amazing accessories and bedazzling baubles."

"Oh, yeah?" O'Ryan replied, trying hard to keep her head as still as possible. "What kind of bedazzling baubles?"

"Well, in one section of the store I'll sell make-up. Like those great-tasting lip glosses?" Oki said. "I'd make sure to get them in, like, a hundred different flavors."

"That's so *unny-fay*!" O'Ryan replied. "I just

said to Reese earlier today that I really love those tasty glosses."

"And you know what else?" Oki said. "In my store, I'll also have a section where I'll sell those super scented erasers."

"You're reading my mind 'cause I heart them, too!" O'Ryan replied excitedly.

"*And*," Oki said, "in case any boys ever come into the store, I'll also have the gross stuff they like. I'm thinking little robots and stuff that's made out of mud and sticks and whatever."

O'Ryan laughed. This was too hilarious! What Oki was saying was almost exactly what Reese had said only a few hours before.

"Well, good news, Oki! You don't need to wait till you're older to have a store like that, 'cause a school treasurer could do the same thing at our school store."

"You think so?" Oki said. "I mean, maybe I should run for treasurer, then. You know, it's always been my dream to be school treasurer."

"*What*?" O'Ryan asked, trying to turn around again. Problem was, since O'Ryan still couldn't see Oki's face, she couldn't tell if Oki was joking...or not.

"Well, I mean, sure. It makes sense," Oki said, holding up her pointer finger. "First of all, I'm the shopper's shopper. I know exactly what I'd put in that school store of ours! Second," she added, extending her middle finger and adding it to her pointer,  "if you think about it, no one spends money better than me. Seriously, just take a look around." She waved her arms around her room. Then, leaving the rest of O'Ryan's hair undone, Oki picked up one of her coats, then some of the objects on her dresser: a big flamenco fan with feathers on it, a beautiful multi-colored seashell, and a picture frame decorated with ruby rhinestones.

No doubt about it, Oki truly was a super-star shopper.

"Then, of course, there's this," Oki added, marching over toward her bed.

On the wall, Oki had made a collage out of all the store receipts she'd ever collected. Funny, the design looked very similar to Reese's dollar-bill wallpaper!

"But third and most important," Oki exclaimed, holding up her third finger and forming the tri-fingered Girl Scout pledge, "you—my best friend in the Whole Wide World—also think it's a good idea for me to run for treasurer. So that just seals the deal. I'll do it!"

Ho.

Lee.

Cow!

"You should run for school secretary, instead!" O'Ryan blurted out, quickly throwing her hands up, as if she were trying to stop a runaway train.

"School secretary?" Oki replied, walking over to her collection of lip glosses and painting some Blueberry Bananarama on her lips. "Why in the *world* would I want to run for that?"

"Uh," O'Ryan said, thinking as quickly as she could, "because you have the best handwriting of anyone I know!"

"So what? Who cares?" Oki replied. "What does that have to do with the price of a pair of purple leggings? We were just talking about how I should be school treasurer!"

"Well, I was just thinking, since you have perfect penmanship," O'Ryan said, as she nervously ran her finger around her lips, "it would just make sense for you to run for secretary!"

*From the groovy desk of*
*Oki Omoto*
↑
*Fab handwriting!*
*—O'Ryan*

"But I want to be treasurer!" Oki said. "Think about it: a secretary isn't the one who does the buying. And buying is my specialty."

Then something dawned on Oki and the idea took her so much by surprise, she wound up squirting lip gloss on the floor. "Wait a second," Oki gasped, sucking in her breath. "I get it now."

"Get what?"

"You don't think I should run for treasurer because you don't think I can do the job!"

"What? No! No, I didn't say that. I don't even *think* that."

"I bet you're going, like, '*Well, Oki's personal*

*style may be white-hot and snazzy, but her math skills aren't up to snuff,'"* she said.

"Oki, that's not what I think at all!" O'Ryan said, her half-braided hair now sticking out of her head in several directions.

"So you *don't* think my personal style is white-hot and snazzy?"

"No, that's not what I'm saying, either!"

"Then what in the world *do* you mean!?" Oki asked, starting to look as frazzled as O'Ryan's hair.

O'Ryan looked at her best friend in the Whole Wide World and realized there was no way she could explain it. So O'Ryan did the only thing she could think of that would make her friend feel better.

"Oki," O'Ryan said, grabbing her BF by the wrist. "I think you'd make the most supreme school treasurer imaginable."

"Really?" Oki replied, a smile starting to light up her face.

"*Eally-ray,*" O'Ryan replied.

O'Ryan hoped the fact she'd just responded in Pig Latin would somehow make her less blameworthy for saying EXACTLY the same thing to Oki that she had said to her twin sister, Reese, just a few hours earlier.

"And, of course, you'll be my campaign manager," Oki said.

"Ure-say," replied O'Ryan.

Clearly, O'Ryan's answers sounded good to Oki. And Oki showed just how happy they made her by pulling her best friend into a huge hug.

## Chapter 3

# That's the Way the Cookie Crumbles

"**G**uess what, Groovy Girls?" Vanessa said at lunch the next day at school.

"You've discovered what the lunch ladies really mean by 'mystery meat'?" Gwen asked, poking her fork into the dry lump on her plate.

"No," Vanessa laughed. "I wanted to tell you

that I've made a woolly-mammoth whopper of a decision. It's about something that's been a dream of mine for years."

*...woolly-mammoth whopper of a decision?*

*...a dream for years?*

O'Ryan suddenly got a sticky-icky feeling in her stomach. And it had nothing to do with the mysterious meat that was sitting in front of Gwen. It was because those words sounded too familiar.

*No! This absolutely, positively cannot be happening!* O'Ryan thought to herself. It was like hearing the song you hated most on the radio playing again and again...and again!

"I want to be your next school president!" Vanessa said triumphantly.

"President?!" O'Ryan repeated, just to confirm. "You're running for president?"

"That's right!" Vanessa replied.

O'Ryan was so Thrilled (with a capital T) that Vanessa wasn't also going to be running for treasurer, she could barely control her excitement.

"Vanessa!" O'Ryan yelled, jumping up from the table. "That's super-supreme! That's the bee's knees, the cat's pajamas, and the elephant's eyebrows all rolled into one! You'll make such an amazing president. You're just what this school needs!"

"That's what I told her!" Yvette said, patting Vanessa on the arm. "Which is part of the reason why she made me her campaign manager. Well, that, and the fact that I'm her best friend."

Oki smiled at O'Ryan and gave her a little nod. It was a nod that said, "That's why you're *my* campaign manager, too." And it was the same nod and smile that Reese was giving O'Ryan at the same time.

"Anyway," Yvette continued, "you should hear all the good ideas I already have for the campaign."

"Like what?" Reese asked.

"Do tell!" Oki added.

Before announcing that they were running for treasurer, both Reese and Oki were thinking they could get some good ideas for their campaigns.

"Well, I was thinking that Vanessa should tell everyone that if she's elected, she'll put soda in the water fountains," Yvette replied.

"Ooh, I like that!" Gwen said. "That's very funky."

"And I think Vanessa should also promise people that if they vote for her, she'll make sure they don't get homework on the weekends," Yvette continued.

"Sounds good." Vanessa nodded. "But, uh, can I really make that happen?"

"Who cares?" Yvette replied, taking a big bite out of her apple. "As long as it gets you elected."

"Okay then!" Vanessa said, beaming at Yvette. "How lucky am I to have a campaign manager like her, huh?"

"And guess what!" Reese said.

"And guess what!" Oki said.

"I'm running for school treasurer!"

"JINX!" Gwen laughed because both Reese and Oki had said the same thing at the same time.

But Gwen was the only one laughing. Because everyone else's mouths had dropped open into giant O's—as in Uh-Oh!

"*You're* running for treasurer?" Reese asked Oki.

"Yeah," Oki replied. "You're running for treasurer, too?" And then she added: "I thought O'Ryan would have told you. She's my campaign manager, after all."

"*What?*" Reese said, dropping her peanut-butter crackers. "She can't be *your* campaign manager, Oki, because O'Ryan already volunteered to be MY campaign manager. She even promised me, didn't you, O'Ryan?"

All eyes at the table turned to O'Ryan. And O'Ryan's eyes turned to the ground.

"Is it true, O'Ryan?" Vanessa asked.

"Uh," O'Ryan replied, not quite knowing what else to say. She looked back and forth between her twin and her best friend.

"How could this have happened?" Reese said, standing up.

"Why didn't you tell me about this before?" Oki added, also rising.

"Whose campaign manager *are* you?" both girls said together.

"JI—" Gwen started to squeal, but when she looked at the serious expressions on the faces of all the others, she didn't finish the jinx.

Still, jinx or no jinx, everyone was silent. And if ever there was a need for a leader, it was now—and Vanessa stepped right in to lead.

"Wait a second, wait a second, hold the cell

phone," Vanessa said, standing up and putting a hand on the shoulders of both Reese and Oki, encouraging them to sit back down again. "Know what I just remembered? Today's my day to do dessert for the table, and I can't think of a better time to hand out some sweetness than right now! So sit right down, and I'll start circulating the cookies." Vanessa reached into her knapsack and produced a giant Ziploc bag, which she held up in front of the Groovies.

And now, dangling before them, in Vanessa's clear plastic baggie, were the most outrageously intense-looking chocolate-chip-chunk cookies you'd ever seen. They were the kind of cookies that made you forget your problems—which was exactly the effect Vanessa was hoping they'd have.

"One for you," Vanessa said, handing the first cookie to Yvette. "One for each of you," she said, handing out cookies to Reese and Oki

at the same time. "And one for Gwen and one for O'Ryan."

"Mmmmm," Gwen said, as the perfectly home-made cookie dissolved on her tongue. "Vanessa, if you promise to keep baking cookies like this, I'll vote for you every day!"

"Now *there's* a great idea, Gwen!" Yvette said, a smile spreading across her face.

"What is?" Gwen asked, chocolate chip goo spreading across hers.

"I bet everyone would vote for Vanessa in exchange for one of her specially baked Vanessa for Prez cookies. What do you think, 'Nessa?"

"Yvette, you are one smart cookie!" Vanessa laughed, and the girls high-fived.

But as soon as Reese finished her cookie, her hands went right back to her hips. "So, what are we gonna do about the fact that both Oki and I are running for treasurer *and* that O'Ryan promised both of us she'd be our campaign manager?"

"Yeah!" Oki said, finishing her cookie and wiping her mouth with a napkin. "What *are* we going to do?"

"People!" Gwen said, pausing and waiting to make sure she had everyone's attention. "I've got a great idea. *I'll* be Reese's campaign manager.

I mean, I'm your best friend, right?" she said, looking at Reese.

Reese nodded.

"So it makes perfect sense that I should be running your campaign!" Gwen continued. "That way all the best friends will be running the campaigns."

Now Gwen assumed that when Reese heard her very generous offer, she'd be in seventh heaven sitting on cloud nine. After all, Gwen was a real rah-rah girl. And when she got behind something or someone, she worked like crazy for the cause.

But when Reese finally said something, it was just this:

"Okay, I guess. Thanks, Gwen."

It wasn't that Reese wasn't grateful. It was that Reese was still so stunned by the news that O'Ryan had jumped ship—had bailed out of *her* ship and

had jumped onto the S.S. *Oki*—that she couldn't yet think about anything else.

And because there was a big-sister issue at play. In fact, it was a "is my big sister really going to campaign *against* me?!" issue.

Likewise, O'Ryan's stomach was twisting and turning in knots. It was as if she were being asked to choose between getting a pony and taking a trip around the world.

And, as everyone knows, no one should have to make that choice!

"My brain must be a light-bulb factory today, 'cause I just got another bright idea!" Yvette laughed. "I'm seeing a Groovy Girls sleepover where we can all make campaign posters, pins, and banners to help each other out. It'll be a blast, and we can all work together, you know?"

"Yeah, if we work together that would be great!" Vanessa said.

"And that way, I'll be able to help *both* Reese and Oki," O'Ryan nodded.

"And," Yvette added, "we can make the cookies we'll need to get Vanessa elected president!"

As the girls laughed, O'Ryan again looked between Reese and Oki to see what they thought of the idea.

Reese was smiling but her lips were pressed together.

Oki was smiling, too, but she was rubbing her forehead with her fingers.

And although both candidates for treasurer were sitting on opposite sides of O'Ryan—and although both clearly wanted to win—at that moment they completely understood how the other one was feeling.

## Chapter 4

# Flour Power!

"That's one of the official 'Reese McCloud for Treasurer' pencils, isn't it?" Reese asked O'Ryan at the sleepover on Saturday night, as the girls sat in their living room making campaign posters.

O'Ryan looked down at the fancy pencil, then back up at Reese. "Sure is!" she replied. "And it writes great!"

Reese for Treas!

"I know!" Reese said, grabbing it away from her sister. "So it should ONLY be used for official Reese McCloud for Treasurer poster-making activities."

In fact, the slogan O'Ryan was writing read: "Oki's No Jokey for Treasurer!"

"Reese, you're kidding, right? You *seriously* don't want me to be using your pencil just because I'm working on one of Oki's posters?" O'Ryan asked.

"Serious as a bad haircut," Reese replied.

Overhearing the conversation, Oki walked over to O'Ryan.

"Here ya go, O'Ryan," Oki said, handing her BFF a fantastic gold-glitter pen. "I think you should be using *this* pen, anyway, when you're doing my posters. It's *way* better than Reese's pencil. And I want people to know that I'm going to be golden as their treasurer. So just give Reese her regular old pencil back."

It had been like this—as uncomfortable as an itchy shirt tag rubbing against your neck—since the sleepover started.

When Oki had arrived, for instance, she'd asked

O'Ryan to help her come up with some slammin' slogans. But Reese had said, "O'Ryan's too busy making pins for me now. Try again later."

*Then*, when O'Ryan was making posters for Oki, and Reese had asked her sister if she'd listen to her why-you-should-vote-for-me speech, Oki had replied, "Sorry, but O'Ryan's too busy concentrating on *my* posters to listen to *you* right now."

Even though Vanessa was usually the one to make peace between the girls, it was Gwen who stepped in to stop the Great Pencil Hullabaloo. "Hey, O'Ryan," Gwen called out. "Toss me that 'Reese' pencil, okay? I need to use it on this super-cool banner I'm making for her."

Gwen was surrounded by lots of unusual art supplies, everything from newspaper to streamers to thick pieces of chalk to multi-colored glue sticks.

"What've you got going on over there?" O'Ryan asked.

"Only the most original campaign poster EVER!" Gwen said. "I just want to make sure Reese has a banner that's as wildly wonderful as she is. How're your posters coming, Vanessa?"

"Delish!" Vanessa replied proudly, holding up a poster that she'd cut into a giant circle to make it look like a chocolate chip cookie. The poster read:

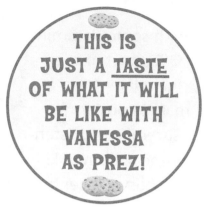

THIS IS JUST A <u>TASTE</u> OF WHAT IT WILL BE LIKE WITH VANESSA AS PREZ!

"And what's up with the cookie production?" Vanessa asked her campaign manager, who had just come in from the kitchen.

"I just put another batch on the cooling racks," Yvette answered, "and Mrs. McCloud put cookie sheet number four into the oven!"

"How many cookies do you think you need to make?" Reese asked.

"Well, we're trying to make at least one cookie for everyone in school," Vanessa replied. "Which means we need to bake exactly 1,057!"

When Yvette started back to the kitchen, all the other girls joined her. (After all, it wasn't easy resisting the smell of freshly baked chocolate chip cookies!)

But when the girls got to the kitchen, there wasn't much cookie counting to be done. Because as it turned out, they weren't the *only* ones who'd been hypnotized by the smell of cookies baking: Sleepless, the McCloud's "innocent" little puppy, had, too!

And he was in the process of helping himself to as many cookies as he could get his paws on.

"Sleepless, no!" O'Ryan said, trying to save a few of the remaining cookies from the dog's roving tongue. "Look what you've done. And you're gonna get sick, too!"

The little dog wagged his tail, seeming to say that even if he *did* get sick, it was worth it! The girls walked back into the living room, not knowing what to do next.

"Okay, Groovy Girls," Vanessa said, taking charge. "We're just gonna have to start over and kick things into high gear! I think we can all use a break from poster-making anyway, so why don't we pitch in and see how many cookies we can bake if we all do it together!"

"Before we do that, though," Gwen said excitedly, "come check out my banner!"

Everyone looked to see the big poster Gwen had been working on all evening.

"Ta-*da*!" she said proudly.

When Reese looked down, her mouth dropped open.

In the middle of the sheet, Gwen had pasted,

in all types of different lettering, "ReESe fOr TrEAsuRer." It was a multi-colored, multi-medium jumble in which she had used every piece of scrap paper, construction paper, and newspaper that she'd found. To say the least, this was *not* a traditional campaign banner.

Which Gwen thought was a great thing.

Which Reese thought was an eyesore!

"Gwen, what's *that* supposed to be?" Reese asked, pointing to the banner. "I mean, it's really creative and all, but it's kind of a mess."

Gwen looked at her banner again. Reese was right: It *was* kind of messy. But she thought that was part of its cool-osity and charm. Plus, she'd worked really hard on it. And it would have been nice if Reese had at least pretended to like it.

"Time to make the cookies!" Vanessa said, seeing the look of disappointment in Gwen's eye. She grabbed Gwen's hand and pulled her toward the kitchen.

"I'll get the extra mixing bowls," O'Ryan shouted.

"Where are your wooden spoons?" Oki asked.

"Middle drawer," Reese replied.

"Okay, good news is we've got plenty of vanilla, sugar, and chocolate chips left!" Yvette said. She handed out different ingredients to each girl.

"Flour power!" Gwen said, reaching into the bag she'd been given and throwing a handful of the white stuff in Reese's direction.

Reese squealed as the white cloud of powder settled all over her clothes. "Okay, I guess I deserved that," she said to Gwen. "And I should have told you how much I appreciate your help."

"Thank you," Gwen said, feeling better already. Then, just to show she was over it, Gwen reached her hand into the bag of flour again and tossed a little in the direction of all the other girls, too!

Soon enough, everyone was caked in white powder. Then they got to work cracking eggs, adding sugar, and stirring, rolling, and scooping their way through batches of Vanessa for Prez cookie batter. We won't even discuss all the licking of spoons and bowls that was going on....

"Oh, *man*, if I eat one more chocolate chip my belly might burst," Vanessa said.

"Isn't this cookie idea the best?" Yvette replied.

"Totally," Oki agreed. "And, you know, if I

weren't running against Reese, I might suggest she start baking some campaign cookies for herself. But instead of using chocolate chips, she could use Reese's pieces."

The suggestion was completely inspired!

"Oki, that's a fantastically smart idea," Reese replied. "I mean, would you mind if I…"

Oki smiled back at Reese. "Of course I don't mind," she said. "We're friends, aren't we? So that's why I mentioned it."

"And maybe you could make Ore-O-ki cookies!" Reese replied.

"Oh, that's outrageous, Reese, thanks!" Oki replied.

"Okay, well, before we switch from chocolate chips," Vanessa interrupted, "let's see how many more cookies we need to make for *me*."

"Girls," Yvette said, "there's some good news and some bad news here."

"What's the good news?" Reese asked.

"Good news is we've baked about a hundred cookies already."

Whoa…

"What's the bad news?" Oki asked.

"We still have about nine hundred fifty-seven to go!"

Whoa...

"I don't know if I can do this anymore," Gwen replied.

"Me neither," said Reese, throwing down her towel.

"But we *have* to!" Yvette said. "We want to get Vanessa elected, don't we?"

The girls looked at Vanessa. Well, sure they wanted her to become president, but...

Vanessa shook her head. "We can't keep this up," she said wisely.

"But why would everyone vote for you if you aren't going to give everyone cookies?" Yvette asked.

"Well, I'm going to be voting for her because I think she's a great leader," O'Ryan volunteered.

"And I'm gonna vote for her because I think she'll get things done," Oki said.

"I'll vote for her because I think she's really smart," Reese added. "And it's important for a president to be smart!"

"Me," Gwen said, "well, I'll tell you why I'll vote for her. I think she's the grooviest candidate around."

Oki and Reese both shot Gwen a look.

"For president!" Gwen added quickly. "She's the grooviest candidate for president, okay?"

Both candidates for treasurer nodded.

"So, can we get out of the kitchen now," Gwen asked, "and get to our pizza?"

"Your future president thinks that's a stupendous idea!" Vanessa replied.

O'Ryan carried in the pizza that had been delivered earlier and plunked it down on the living room floor so everyone could grab their slices. Reese and Oki both reached for large cheesy pieces, and then they looked at each other and smiled.

Sure, of course they were running against each other, but they were still good friends, right?

Sure...but...

"Here, O'Ryan," Oki said. "I want you to have this slice."

"No!" Reese exclaimed. "I got this slice specially for you."

The girls each held out their slice, waiting to see which one O'Ryan would take. The problem was, both Oki and Reese's slices looked good. But O'Ryan knew if she took Oki's slice, Reese would be upset. And if she took Reese's slice, Oki would get miffed. O'Ryan just couldn't choose between them, so she said the only thing she could.

"Uh, I actually don't think I'll have either one. Suddenly, I'm just not that hungry."

"Really?" Gwen said. "Well then, let me help you out there, O'Ryan." Gwen reached for *both* slices. "Lucky for you—and for me—I always have room for extra pizza!"

P.S. This time, Sleepless, who loved pizza, too, was in the same spot as O'Ryan—but for his own reasons. Too many cookies had made for one stuffed pup!

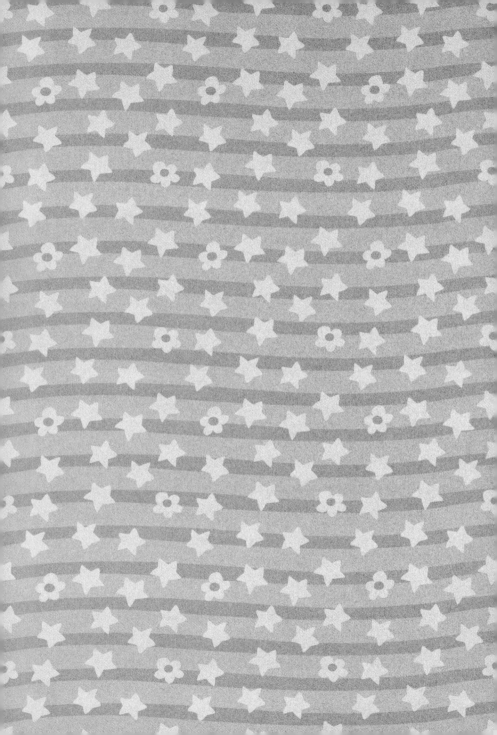

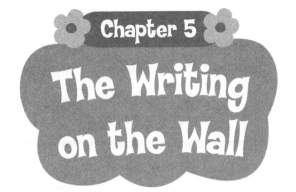

# Chapter 5

# The Writing on the Wall

"Oh, *there* you are!" Reese said, walking into the art room Monday after school. "I've been looking all over for you!"

"Really?" O'Ryan replied, trying to sound as innocent as possible.

But the fact that Reese had been looking for her didn't really surprise O'Ryan at all.

Why? Because O'Ryan had been hiding from her!

After the sleepover Saturday night, O'Ryan knew she needed to get away. And she finally thought she'd found that place in the art room. In fairness, it wasn't just Reese whom O'Ryan had been hiding from, it was also—

"Oh, *there* you are!" Oki said, fluttering into the art room a few moments later. "O'Ryan, I've been trying to track you down ever since the bell rang!"

"Gee, I had no idea," O'Ryan said, again trying to act surprised.

"Hey, what're you doing?" Reese asked, looking at the sheet of butcher paper that O'Ryan had painted with red and white stripes.

"I'm doing a 'Choose or Lose' poster," O'Ryan replied.

"Really?" Oki asked. "Why?"

"Because it's important to remind people that their vote counts," O'Ryan said. "That if they want to have a say in what goes on at school, they've got to cast a ballot."

O'Ryan had taken a paintbrush and dipped it in a can of black paint and was carefully writing the words "Get Out and Vote!" across the poster.

"So, who are you telling people to vote for?" Reese asked.

"Yeah, who?" Oki said, sounding every bit as interested.

Naturally, each candidate for treasurer was hoping that the poster would be in support of her.

"It's not for anyone in particular," O'Ryan replied. "It's like a public service announcement."

"What?" Reese asked.

"Like the ones they have on TV," O'Ryan said with authority, as she continued painting. "You know, the ones that don't sell a product, just a good idea. Like how reading aloud to your kids makes them smarter."

"Oh, yeah," Oki nodded.

"So, what's the good idea you're selling?" Reese asked.

"Like I said, that voting's important," O'Ryan replied. "And smart!"

The candidates let this sink in for a moment.

"Well, you know what?" Oki finally responded. "I think that's a great idea, O'Ryan!"

"Yeah," Reese agreed. "It *is* a duper-super scheme."

"Like *I* said," Oki added, "it's a peach of a proposal."

"Yup," Reese nodded, "it'll be the apple of their eyes!"

"Thank you, thank you," O'Ryan replied, putting her hands in the air to let the girls know she had heard them. "I mean, I just figured if I did a poster like this, it would help you both."

Oki smiled. "That's so nice of you," she said, picking up a paintbrush. "And I would be so happy to help you."

"Yeah, let me help, too!" Reese added. "And here, let me get you a new paintbrush."

"Thanks," O'Ryan replied, pleasantly surprised by the girls' enthusiasm, and happy that Oki and Reese would finally be working *together* again— instead of *against* each other.

Reese came back from the supply closet carrying two brushes. One for her, one for O'Ryan, none for Oki. So much for working together!

"I'll just go get a brush of my own," Oki said in response.

When she came back, Oki looked at the poster and tried to figure out how best to make her contribution. She smiled as she added two extra words next to O'Ryan's "Get Out and Vote!"

And those words were: "for Oki!"

"Wait, let me in!" Reese said. Then, without bothering to let Oki's addition to the poster dry, Reese crossed out the words "for Oki!" and wrote "for Reese!" directly below it.

"Hey!" Oki cried, taking her paintbrush back to the poster and smearing it across Reese's name.

"Look what you did!" Reese cried right back, making a curlicue through Oki's mark and muddying the paint even more.

"Don't do that!" Oki said, as Reese's arm knocked her elbow.

"Watch it!" Reese replied, when Oki let a huge blob of paint drop on her name.

The paint, as they say, had hit the fan.

And the back table.

And the floor.

And the supply cabinets.

"HEY! Knock it off!" O'Ryan finally yelled, looking at the wrecked election poster that her best friend and best twin had just ruined.

Reese and Oki stopped in their Technicolor tracks. Reese looked at Oki and Oki looked at Reese, and they were about to start pointing fingers at each other. But before they got the chance, O'Ryan shook her head. "I can't believe this. Look at the mess you've made here!"

The girls looked...and what they saw wasn't pretty.

"And I'm not just talking about the poster. Look at the mess you've made for me!" O'Ryan continued. "With the two of you running against each other, *I'm* the one in a no-win situation!" She turned to Oki. "How can you expect me to campaign against my very own twin?" she said. Then she turned to Reese. "And how can you expect me to campaign against my very best friend?"

Neither Oki nor Reese had a good answer for the *very* good questions they'd just been asked.

"Did you ever *once* think about how I've been feeling during all this?" O'Ryan added.

The girls shook their heads.

"Yeah, I didn't think so," O'Ryan replied. "Now excuse me, please, but I need to go take a walk."

"Do you want me to come with you?" Reese asked.

"No," O'Ryan answered.

"Do you want *me* to come with you?" Oki added.

"Not that, either," O'Ryan said.

She then turned around and walked out the door, leaving the two girls smack in the middle of the very mess they'd created.

Oki and Reese stood there for a moment, thinking about what O'Ryan had just said, finally putting themselves in her knee-high boots.

"I can't believe we've been trying to make her choose between us," Reese said quietly as she took a sponge from the sink and started wiping up the paint mess.

"We've been as unfair as a rainy day at the carnival," Oki agreed, following behind Reese with a drying rag.

"So," Reese said, "what are we going to do to make this better?"

Oki shrugged her shoulders. "I don't know exactly. But what I *do* know is that I feel big-time-yucky that I've made my best friend mad."

"You didn't mean to, you just got caught up in the excitement," Reese said, nodding at Oki. "So did I."

"Even so," Oki responded, "now we need to figure out a way to show her that—whatever happens during the election for treasurer tomorrow—*she's* the one who we value most."

"Yeah, I think that's smart," Reese agreed. "You know, Oki, if I weren't running against you for treasurer, I'd definitely vote for you."

"Ditto, girl," Oki replied, smiling. "And you

know what else? This whole paint-splatter thing looks kind of good on you." Oki pointed to the flecks of paint that had gotten all over Reese's face.

"On you, too," Reese said, smiling right back. Then—she couldn't resist—she dipped her finger in a puddle of paint and touched it to Oki's nose!

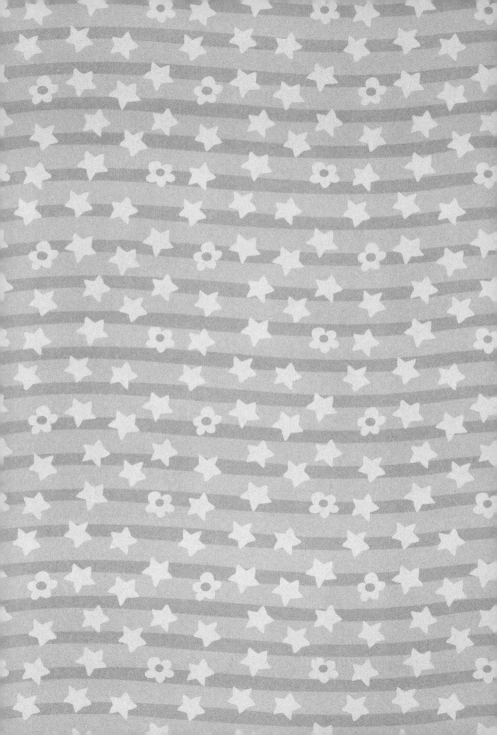

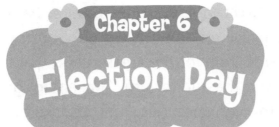

## Chapter 6

# Election Day

"**Y**ou ready, Freddy?" Reese asked Oki as they sat onstage, side by side, during the election assembly the next morning.

Oki nodded. "Ready as set and go!"

While cleaning up their mess in the art room the day before, the girls had thought of how to make things right with O'Ryan. And part of their plan began by sharing the stage like dazzling diplomats.

"Your two candidates for treasurer have made a rather unusual request," the school principal said when it came time for the treasurers to present themselves to the auditorium. "Instead of giving regular campaign speeches, they've asked to debate each other."

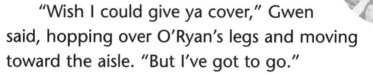

"I hope 'debate' doesn't really mean 'wrestle,'" O'Ryan said to Gwen, who was sitting next to her in the audience. "I don't think I can watch. Hide me!"

"Wish I could give ya cover," Gwen said, hopping over O'Ryan's legs and moving toward the aisle. "But I've got to go."

"You do? Where?" O'Ryan asked.

"You'll see," Gwen answered, as she turned and walked up to the stage. Then she climbed the stairs and moved to the front of the podium, lowering the microphone so it was perfectly at mouth-level.

"PHHHHSHH," she blew into the microphone. "Is this thing on?"

"Yes!" everyone in the audience called back.

"Good," Gwen said. "Hi, everyone. My name is Gwen, and Oki and Reese have asked me to help out with their debate." She continued, "That means I'm the one who gets to ask all the questions!" Then she added, "Oh, hi Vanessa!" giving a little wave to the Groovy Girl who was also sitting up onstage waiting to give her speech for president. "Sorry, I got a little distracted there for a minute," she said, turning back to the audience.

Gwen looked at the two girls who were now standing on each side of her. "Okay, back to business. Now, you should know, the girls haven't heard any of these questions before. And that's basically 'cause I just made them up on the bus to school this morning...*Kidding*!" Gwen said.

Several members of the audience laughed. (They knew Gwen, and knew she probably wasn't really kidding.)

"Anyhowze," Gwen said, "if everyone's ready, let's begin. Okay, the first question goes to Oki. If you're elected treasurer, Oki, what's the first thing you would change about the school store?"

"Well," Oki replied, "I have a *lot* of great ideas for the store, but I'd love to issue school debit cards. That way, if you've put money in your account, you can buy what you need when you need it. With a debit card system, you won't have to carry cash around in your socks anymore. And if you suddenly realize you *must* have a pencil with a Troll top, you'll just be able to go in and charge it!"

"Cool," Gwen said. "Reese, how about you?"

"Well, I think that's actually a great idea," Reese replied, nodding at Oki. "But I guess if I could change only one thing at first, it would be to keep the store open for more hours during the school day so everyone could have more time to shop."

"Yeah," Oki said, "Reese's right about that. I don't think there can ever be enough time to shop!"

"Now that's the Oki we know and love, huh?" Gwen replied. "Okay, now the next question goes to you first, Reese," Gwen said. "As treasurer, how would you raise enough money so that we could have more school field trips to places like space museums and amusement parks?"

"Well, I guess I'd suggest having a bunch of cookie sales to start," Reese replied.

"Which is a really great idea, since Reese would probably bake something incredible like Reese's pieces chocolate chip cookies," Oki said excitedly. "I'm sure she'd be able to raise that money for you in no time."

"Or," Reese added, "if you baked Ore-O-ki cookies, it'd probably rain money in here."

"Cool beans!" Oki said, nodding at her competitor, who was beginning to seem a lot less like a girl running against her and a lot more like the regular old Reese Oki had always appreciated.

"New question for you, Oki," Gwen continued. "Since you're running for treasurer, after all, can you tell everyone what's the *one* thing in the world you'd put the highest price tag on?"

Oki didn't pause for a second. "That's easy," she replied. "You wanna know what I think is so valuable I'd even say it's priceless?" She let the question hang there for a moment.

The audience waited, leaning forward in their seats.

Was she talking about a lah-dee-dah diamond?
A fancy-schmancy designer handbag?
A hoity-toity piece of art?

"Friends," Oki said, looking out into the audience and finding O'Ryan to make eye contact with. "I wouldn't sell my friends for anything, no matter how much you gave me! That's how much they're worth to me."

"Zuper-cool! What about you, Reese?" Gwen asked, turning to her best friend.

"All I can say is that I second that answer," Reese replied. "And I'd like to add that, based on Oki's answers to the questions you've just asked, I think it's pretty obvious she'd make a terrific treasurer."

"And Reese," Oki added, "would be a super-supreme treasurer, too!"

"In other words," Gwen said, smiling at both candidates, and then at the audience, "no matter how this election turns out, everyone wins!"

A few more questions went back and forth between the two "dazzlingly diplomatic" candidates for treasurer. But the audience got the gist pretty quickly: Both Oki and Reese were smart and hip would-be treasurers!

And the one member of the audience who was trying to remain as neutral as possible—aka O'Ryan—turned out to clap the loudest when the girls bowed together at the end of their great debate.

## Chapter 7

# And the Winner Is...

"We tied!" Reese and Oki exclaimed to Gwen, O'Ryan, and Yvette in the cafeteria the following day at lunch.

"Say what?" Yvette asked.

"Yeah," Reese replied, "they just finished counting the votes."

"We split 'em down the middle," Oki said. "So the same number of people that thought

Reese was the right girl for the job thought I was the right one, too."

"So, what are you guys going to do?" Gwen asked.

"Does this mean there'll be a run-off?" Yvette added.

O'Ryan held her breath. The thought of Oki and Reese starting the whole campaign process over again made her head hurt.

"Nope, no run-off!" Oki replied. "We decided that we're going to be co-treasurers!"

"Co-treasurers?" O'Ryan repeated, hoping she'd heard right.

"Co-treasurers," Reese confirmed. "We realized that even though Oki and I are really different—"

"And we've got gazillions of different ideas," Oki said, interrupting.

"If we work together, we can be, like, twice as good!"

"Which, in treasurer's terms, means we're gonna give this school a whole lot more bang for its buck!" Oki added.

"So it turns out you're *both* winners," Gwen said. "And you're both the right girl for the job."

"Which I think is the very definition of the term Win-Win," O'Ryan said, smiling like she, herself, was the big winner of the day.

And speaking of winners, that's when Vanessa strode into the cafeteria. Reaching out to Reese and Oki she said, "President Vanessa congratulates you both!"

"YAY!" Yvette said, jumping up to hug her best friend on her victory. "So you won? You really won?!"

"Hugely," Vanessa said to Yvette. "But I don't want to brag."

"And as one of your co-treasurers, I just want to say it will be with the greatest pleasure that I'll look forward to working with you," Oki pronounced rather formally.

"Ditto," Reese said.

"So you know what this means, right?" Vanessa asked. "I want my two treasurers to start raising money for our special-projects fund right away."

The two co-treasurers nodded at each other. They were thrilled to get started and excited to show everyone—especially O'Ryan—that they could work together brilliantly!

"Know what we should do?" Reese said, her eyes widening.

"What?" Oki asked, excited that inspiration had already struck within the first few seconds of their new and powerful partnership.

"We should start selling some of those 100 cookies that we baked for Vanessa's campaign."

"You're kidding, right?" Oki asked. "We can't do that!"

"Why not?" Reese said.

"Well, those cookies are, like, four days old already," Oki replied, shaking her head.

"I've eaten week-old cookies," Gwen said. "And they're not so bad, if you like stale stuff."

Reese nodded at her best friend. "See that?" she said. "I say we sell 'em."

"Not on my watch," Oki said, crossing her arms in front of her chest.

"What do you think, O'Ryan?" both girls asked at the same time.

But O'Ryan quickly jammed a big bite of sandwich in her mouth, holding up her hands to indicate she couldn't reply.

"I think she's saying it's impolite to talk with her mouth full," Yvette translated.

O'Ryan tapped her finger to her nose and nodded.

Then Oki looked at Reese, and Reese looked at Oki, and they both laughed, realizing exactly what they'd done.

"You know, O'Ryan," Oki said, "we *can* wait for you to swallow to tell us who you think is right and who you think is wrong."

"But the good news," Reese continued, "is that we're not going to do that."

"Yeah," Oki nodded, "we'll figure it out by ourselves."

"I could help!" Gwen chimed in. "I mean, I'd be happy to sample as many of those cookies as you need to see if they're still okay."

"Thanks, but I'm sure Reese will eventually realize that I'm right," Oki replied smiling. "Selling stale cookies is just bad beeswax!"

"But, remember," Reese replied, smiling just as hard, "there's only one kind of beeswax that's bad beeswax. And that's *no beeswax at all!*"

O'Ryan could see that the great debate between the treasurers would continue. But— this time that was okay with her. After all, they had been here before, and she was sure she could finally let the chocolate chips fall where they may.

# Groovy Girls™
## sleepover handbook

**5**

## LEADER of the PACK QUIZ
### Are You Ready to Run For Prez?

## Time-Out
### 8 GREAT WAYS TO CHILL

**AMAZING CHOCOLATE CHIP CAMPAIGN COOKIES**
Plus Supreme Ice-Cream Sandwiches & Chocolate Chip Pizza!

# Contents

Text by Julia Marsden
Illustrations by Yancey Labat, Bill Alger, Doug Day, Kurt Marquart, Elaine de la Mata

# A Groovy Greeting

## HEY, GROOVY GIRL!

It's time to grab a paintbrush, poster board, banners, and buttons—cuz we're getting ready for our school elections! The Groovies have been super-busy helping me run for prez, and I hope you'll vote for me, too!

So, are you ready to hop on the campaign trail for some awesome adventures? Then read on!

Whether you're running for president, like me, or just being your fab self with your best buds, the one thing you need is confidence! And you can start showing off your pizzaz-zy personality with an Express Yourself Sleepover (see pages 4–5).

With all the buzz about school elections, you might be wondering what kind of leader you are. Do you have the right stuff to be prez? Or is running for treasurer, like Oki and Reese, more your style? Turn to pages 8–10 for a quiz that'll give you the lowdown on your leadership skills!

And what would a sleepover be without a slice of pizza paradise? Turn to page 11 for a perfect pizza recipe that's sure to please all your sleepover buds (and your taste buds, too!). And even though I've had my fill of cookies lately (let's just say the elections have made all of us Groovies a little chocolate-chipped-out), don't miss my very own chocolate chip cookie recipe on page 12. After one bite, you're gonna be cuckoo for chocolate chips and totally ready for more chip-a-licious treats on page 13. Yum-meee!

So, whether you're in a race for school office or just racin' home to plan your next sleepover—here's wishing you lots of groovy good luck! See you at campaign headquarters!

Love Ya, Groovy Girl!
Vanessa

# Throw an Express Yourself
# SLEEPOVER

**SUPREMELY PIZZAZ-ZY!**

**DIVA IN CHARGE!**

**FABULOUSLY FASHIONABL...**

**W**ant to fill up on fun? Plan a game-filled sleepover that'll give you and your friends a chance to get to know each other better, pose plenty of questions, and talk up a storm. In other words...express yourself! Here are a handful of games to get the party started.

## Take Me to Your Leader

**Have each of your guests write on a slip of paper a situation a leader might find herself in.** Place the slips of paper into a hat. Then take turns drawing a slip from the hat and acting out the situation charades-style. A few situations to get things started might include: making a speech, handing out campaign buttons, or running a meeting.

## Friendship 4-1-1

**Are you coming across loud and clear with all that you have to say?** Play a game of telephone and see how mixed up your messages can get when they're not passed along in exactly the same way they got started! For an added element of message mix-up, see what happens when you start a message using O'Ryan's specialty: Pig Latin! *Ound-say ike-lay un-fay?*

# The Chips Are In

**Learn more about your friends by playing The Chips Are In.**
Pass out ten chocolate chips (or jelly beans or M&M's®) to each player. Then each guest should reveal something she's never done before but would like to do. If other players in the group have done it, they get to eat one chocolate chip. Keep playing until someone has "cashed in" (or eaten) all her chips! Some sample statements:

- I've never baked chocolate chip cookies.
- I've never run for school office.
- I've never seen the Statue of Liberty in person.
- I've never had piano lessons.
- I've never performed in a band.
- I've never given a speech before a big audience.

# Fast Five

**Think Fast! How well do you and your friends really know each other?** Play a round of Fast Five and find out. Hand out slips of paper to each of your friends and have them answer five questions like the examples listed below, and sign their names. Then hand over the folded slips of paper to someone who's not playing the game so that the handwriting doesn't give away any clues. Have that person read the answers aloud and then, on other slips of paper, have each player cast their votes for who the person being described is. Once all of the Fast Five lists have been read and you've all cast your votes, find out who matched the most Fast Five lists to their rightful owners. Some Sample questions:

- What's your favorite hobby?
- What's your favorite subject in school?
- What do you like most about yourself?
- Who do you admire most?
- What do you want to be when you grow up?

# GET THE WORD OUT!

**W**hen it comes to expressing yourself, you can pump up the volume of your voice, or even speak in Pig Latin. But there are plenty of other groovylicious ways to get your point across and create some cool crafts at the same time.

Stop 'em at the door with a doorknob hanger that gets your message across. *Keep Out* and *Do Not Disturb* can give way to *Groovy Girls Xing*, *Party Central*, or *Dream On*. Just add peel-and-stick foam letters to a foam door hanger you get at a crafts store, or trace your own door hanger design onto a file folder and cut it out. Use markers to make your statement on one side (or use both sides for double the message).

Start with inspirational words to describe yourself or a friend, and attach them to a small cardboard box with glue. Look through old magazines and clip out words that sum up how you see yourself or a friend. Then use craft glue or a glue stick to place the words randomly on a small cardboard box. Keep it to stash sentimental stuff, or use it to present a pal with a small just-because-you're-you gift.

String small alphabet beads onto a leather cord to create a bracelet that has something to say. *Dream*, *Celebrate*, *Imagine*, or *Believe* are just a few of the possible words you can choose to wrap around your wrist.

Spell out something special with the flat letter tiles from a game such as Scrabble® that's already missing some of its pieces. Glue the names, words, or title you've spelled out with the tiles onto a flat wooden frame, or a frame you make from sturdy cardboard. Then insert the photo in your letter-perfect picture frame.

# Best Friends, Ballots, and Behind-the-Scene SECRETS

Is your name on the ballot, as well as your bud's? Can you take part in school elections without being a candidate? Read on for solutions to cure your campaign blues!

## Ballot Buds

*My friend and I are both running for class president. Can we still stay friends?*

It may be hard not to feel competitive with your friend, but there's no reason why you and your bud can't remain friends. Run a strong campaign and, if you win the election, think about asking your friend if she'd like to share her ideas for making the job the best it can be. If your friend wins, congratulate her as warmly as you would want her to congratulate you. No matter what the outcome is, you and your friend can cast a huge vote in favor of friendship by being supportive of each other. That way, long after all the votes are counted, the friendship you two share will still be going strong.

## Behind-the-Scene Bud

*I'm not big on being a candidate in my school elections. Is there anything else I can do to get involved?*

Being a candidate isn't for everyone, but that doesn't mean you have to be left without a role during your school elections. Why not cast yourself as a campaign manager like Yvette? You can come up with poster slogans, decorate banners, and get ideas from other classmates about what they want to see in a school president or treasurer. Just remember, those confident candidates need lots of help from incredibly involved behind-the-scene buds like you!

7

# Leader of the Pack Quiz

## What Kind of Leader Are You?

You don't need to have a Vanessa-like vibe and run for class president to impress people with your winning style. There are lots of ways to make an impact. What role might be right for you? Take this quiz and then turn to page 10 to find out!

**1. I'm someone who:**

a) plans things out ahead of time. I know exactly how I want my next sleepover to be.

b) loves the limelight. Hand me a microphone and I'm all about amazing the audience!

c) likes to total up numbers...the number of friends to invite to my next sleepover, the number of snacks to serve, the number of games to play.

d) likes to put my thoughts down on paper. I'm the first to write down funny stories my friends tell me, and strange dreams I have.

**2. I feel lost without:**

a) a calendar filled with all kinds of pizzaz-zy plans and exciting events.

b) all my best buds by my side.

c) enough money to buy an awesome accessory for a new outfit.

d) a way to express how I feel—like being able to talk to friends, write in my journal, or draw some sketches.

8

**3.** When I go to the movies, I tend to focus on:

   a) all the details...the scenery, the wardrobes, the props, the lighting.

   b) the stars of the show.

   c) how the characters spend their money.

   d) the script and what the characters are saying.

**4.** My ultimate field trip experience would be:

   a) a behind-the-scene tour of the White House.

   b) going to city hall to meet the mayor.

   c) visiting a hip new music store or boutique to see how they make money.

   d) hanging out for a day with the editor of my fave magazine.

**5.** When it comes to planning a sleepover, you'd love to hear your friends say to you:

   a) Can you be in charge of picking a theme?

   b) Can you be in charge of entertainment?

   c) Can you be in charge of figuring out the food and decorations?

   d) Can you be in charge of creating some cool invitations?

**6.** Your sports team looks to you to:

   a) boost team morale.

   b) score the winning points.

   c) figure out team stats.

   d) write a great team thank-you note to your coach at the end of the season.

**7.** The coolest part of a school election would have to be:

   a) just being part of the whole election scene.

   b) hearing the candidates give their speeches.

   c) the excitement of counting the votes.

   d) the coverage of the whole campaign in class and in the school paper.

# What Do Your **Answers Reveal** About Your
# LEADERSHIP STYLE?

*Voting Box*

### Add up your "votes" and find
### out where you come up a winner!

✸**If you answered mostly A's, why not be a campaign manager?**

Detail-oriented and big on planning, you'd be a great
campaign manager! Just like Yvette, you've got a real
knack for helping your friends shine. Not bothered
by a behind-the-scene situation, you help make
things happen with your great ideas and incredible
enthusiasm. As a campaign manager, you can come
up with cool slogans, make pizzaz-zy posters, and
most important—be a supremely supportive friend!

✸**If you answered mostly B's, why not run for class president?**

Always at home in the spotlight, if there's a campaign,
you're likely to be a candidate! Vote for Vanessa? How
about casting that vote in your direction! As a natural-
born leader, you love to inspire others and are great
at motivating just about everybody you meet. As
class president, you can come up with all kinds of
fun activities (school-wide Olympics, a talent show, a cookie-baking
contest) and listen to your classmates' ideas.

✸**If you answered mostly C's, why not run for class treasurer?**

When it comes to dollars and cents, you're a total money
master! Just like Reese and Oki, you're a pro at spending,
saving, and keeping track of numbers. If there's a cash
crisis, you're there on the scene with lots of problem-
solving strategies that really count! As a treasurer, you
can keep track of the cash flow at school and come
up with clever new ways to raise funds for sports
teams, field trips, and fab school events!

✸**If you answered mostly D's, why not run for class secretary?**

What would you do without the written word?
You love using language to let others know
how you feel. Through letters you write,
and stories you tell, you're able to inform
and entertain lots of people in your life.

# Pizza Paradise

No matter how you slice it,
pizza's a great sleepover selection.
Cast your vote for the ultimate toppings,
and create a seriously scrumptious snack.

## Personalized Pizzas

*(Makes 4 pizzas)*

### Ingredients:

1 roll of ready-to-bake pizza
  dough or 4 mini pre-made
  pizza crusts

1/4 cup olive oil

1 jar of pizza sauce

1 (8-ounce) package of shredded
  mozzarella cheese

Assorted pizza toppings such
  as sliced pepperoni, sliced
  mushrooms, sliced pitted
  black olives, sliced tomatoes

Utensils: Cookie sheets, bowls,
  spoons, plates

### What You Do:

**1.** Ask an adult to
preheat the oven to
350 degrees F.

**2.** If you're using ready-to-bake pizza
dough, separate the dough into four pieces
and roll and shape them into individual
pizza crusts. Drizzle some olive oil on top
of each pizza dough or pre-made pizza
crust and place them on a cookie sheet.

**3.** Place the assorted pizza toppings
in bowls on the table where your
guests can reach them.

**4.** Have each guest spoon some pizza
sauce onto her pizza dough or crust.
Then she can add some cheese and
her favorite pizza toppings.

**5.** Ask an adult to place the cookie sheet
in the oven. Once the cheese is melted,
which should take about 12 minutes,
the mini pizzas will be ready to eat.

### Try Something Different

If pizza sauce and all those toppings aren't your thing—
try making an all-white pizza! Use the same pizza dough
or pre-made pizza crust noted above and drizzle some olive
oil over it. Then sprinkle on ricotta, grated mozzarella,
provolone, or Parmesan cheese (or a mix of your faves).
Ask an adult to place the pizza in the oven. Let the pizza
bake for about 12 minutes or until all the cheese is melted.

# Chip, Chip, Hooray!

YUMMY! CHOCOLATE CHIPS

## Score some major votes of approval with these winning chocolate chip recipes.

## Vanessa's Choice
### Chocolate Chip Cookies
*(Makes about 2 dozen cookies)*

Win over your friends with these delicious cookies— straight from Vanessa's election campaign!

### Ingredients:
½ cup butter, softened

¼ cup packed brown sugar

½ cup sugar

1 teaspoon vanilla extract

1 egg

1 cup flour

½ teaspoon baking soda

½ teaspoon salt

1 (6-ounce) package of semi-sweet chocolate chips (or you can use milk chocolate, white chocolate, or butterscotch chips, or candy-coated milk chocolate pieces)

Utensils: Measuring cups, measuring spoons, spoon, mixing bowl, wooden spoon, two cookie sheets, fork, spatula, wire rack

### What You Do:

**1.** Have an adult preheat the oven to 350 degrees F.

**2.** Stir the butter, both sugars, vanilla, and egg in a large bowl using a wooden spoon.

**3.** Add in the flour, baking soda, and salt and stir until the dough becomes stiff. You might want to take turns passing the bowl around so that everyone has a chance to mix the ingredients (and so your arm won't get too tired!).

**4.** Stir in the chocolate chips.

**5.** Drop the dough by rounded spoonfuls, about two inches apart, onto an ungreased cookie sheet. Flatten a little bit with a fork.

**6.** Bake about 10 minutes or until the cookies are light brown (the centers will be soft).

**7.** Use a spatula to move the cookies from each cookie sheet to a wire rack to cool.

# Chocolate Chip Ice-Cream Sandwiches

*(Makes 4 ice-cream sandwiches)*

## Ingredients:

8 chocolate chip cookies from the recipe on page 12

8 large spoonfuls of vanilla ice cream

1 cup of chocolate chips

Utensils: Spoon, a sheet of waxed paper, two dinner plates

## What You Do:

**1.** Place two large spoonfuls of softened vanilla ice cream between two chocolate chip cookies.

**2.** Place the chocolate chips on a dinner plate and roll the insides of the cookie sandwich in the chocolate chips (so the chips stick to the ice cream).

**3.** Place the ice-cream sandwich on a waxed paper-covered plate and put it in the freezer until the ice cream hardens.

# Chocolate Chip Pizza

*(Makes 1 pizza)*

## Ingredients:

1 roll of ready-to-bake sugar-cookie dough, such as Pillsbury® cookie dough

1 container of strawberry-flavored cream cheese spread

1 cup of chocolate chips

1 cup of shredded coconut

Cooking spray

Utensils: 12-inch pizza pan, butter knife

**If you just can't get enough of pizza (and chocolate chips!), serve up a dessert pizza by the slice.**

## What You Do:

**1.** Ask an adult to preheat the oven to 350 degrees F.

**2.** Grease a 12-inch pizza pan with cooking spray.

**3.** Flatten and shape the sugar-cookie dough so it fits inside the pizza pan.

**4.** Have an adult place the pan in the oven. Bake for about 10 minutes or until the cookie crust is golden at the edges. Let the cookie crust cool completely.

**5.** Use a butter knife to spread the strawberry-flavored cream cheese on the cooled cookie pizza crust.

**6.** Top the crust with chocolate chips and shredded coconut.

**7.** Keep the pizza refrigerated until ready to serve, and then slice like a regular pizza.

13

# Stress Less

**W**hether you're caught in between two competing buds (or, if you're like O'Ryan, between your twin sister and BFF), or just need time to drift off and dream a little, here are some mellowing moves that can give you the chance to chill out.

♥ **Add some flower power to your room.**
Place a small African violet, marigold, or scented geranium in a spot in your room that gets some light. Or, opt for a more herbal approach and plant some sage, rosemary, or basil seedlings. They're all known for their soothing scents. Another indoor garden option? Small succulent plants like a cactus. Succulents don't need much water—or attention—and they come in all kinds of cool shapes and varieties. Caring for your windowsill garden and watching it grow is super-uplifting. Plus, the very plants you're tending will make your room more groovy.

♥ **Take it outside and blow some bubbles.**
Watch the glossy globes drift off—and picture your problems being carried away with them. You can use a bottle of store-bought bubbles, or make some of your own by mixing 2 cups of warm water with $1/4$ cup of light corn syrup, 1 teaspoon of sugar, and $1/2$ cup of dishwashing liquid. Pour your bubbly brew into a shallow pan and bend a pipe cleaner into a wand, or use a plastic berry basket to create tons of tiny bubbles. (If you're using store-bought bubbles, just use the wand that comes with the bottle.)

♥ **Play with some cappuccino clay.** Kneading, rolling, poking, and shaping can help you work out the kinks in the clay and any stressful feelings you're carrying with you. Plus the scent will remind you of a grown-up cup of coffee. In a bowl, mix 2 cups of